Hoops

To: Myma, Karen, Barbara and Kirby

Hoops

By Carl Birk

Jessica Springfield was known
as a basketball fool.
The ball that she bounced,
was her offensive tool.
She could slice through a defense
and dish to an open player.
The basketball she handled,
was her dragon slayer.

The fates had smiled down upon her,
the day she was born.
They provided her the energy,
until her shoes were all worn.
Jessica Springfield had a
special basketball gift.
When she stepped onto the court,
she gave her team a lift.

You would find her dribbling,
morning, noon and night.
Between her legs, around the back
and hidden from sight.
She studied her hero,
the great Sheryl Swoopes.
Which is why Jessica's
nickname simply was Hoops.

When she headed for the blacktop,
in the local park.
The boys trembled with fear
from morning till dark.
Jessica was the absolute best
player in the town.
No matter the opponent,
she would always take them down

Her school, the Bulldogs,
could only afford a boys' team.
Whose coach had a reputation
of being really mean.
At the team tryouts,
Jessie outplayed the boys best.
With every obstacle she faced,
she passed the test.

The principal observed the action
and Hoops awesome game.
He approached the coach
as he was crossing off her name.
After a heated discussion,
Jess was on the team to stay.
"I'll place her on the roster," coach grumbled,
"but she'll never play."

From that day forward,
the Bulldogs struggled to win.
Her teammates pleaded to the coach,
"Please put Hoops in*!!!*"
She patiently sat on the bench
and studied the adversaries moves.
Hoops prepared for the chance
to help the team improve.

The final game was upon the Bulldogs,
the Maulers they would face.
The Maulers were brutally ugly
and the league's big disgrace.
With two minutes remaining
and the Bulldogs down by eight.
The coach finally relented,
sending Jessie to face her fate.

In a flash Jess dribbled down,
for a quick score.
The crowd got on their feet
with a loud roar.
Within seconds she stole another ball
and found her sweet spot.
For the first time that year,
the team had a shot.

The next Maulers possession,
they were stopped down the court.
The spectators started chanting
and showing their support.
Each teammate was covered
leaving it to the rook.
Surprisingly she scored,
with a perfect sky hook.

Losing by two,
with just seconds to go.
The Bulldogs got the ball back,
for the final blow.
Jessie now faced the Maulers
tip-top star.
A seven-foot monster
with several scars.

"Nothing gets by me," he sneered,
"I'll make your life grim."
Hoops just gave him a wink
and her battle fight grin.
The coach now on his knees
and making a wish.
As Hoops launched a three pointer,
that landed with a swish.

The audience went wild,
as the coach quickly fainted.
The entire town now wanted
Hoops to be sainted.
She mesmerized the opposition,
running figure eight loops.
And will always be remembered,
simply as Hoops.

The End